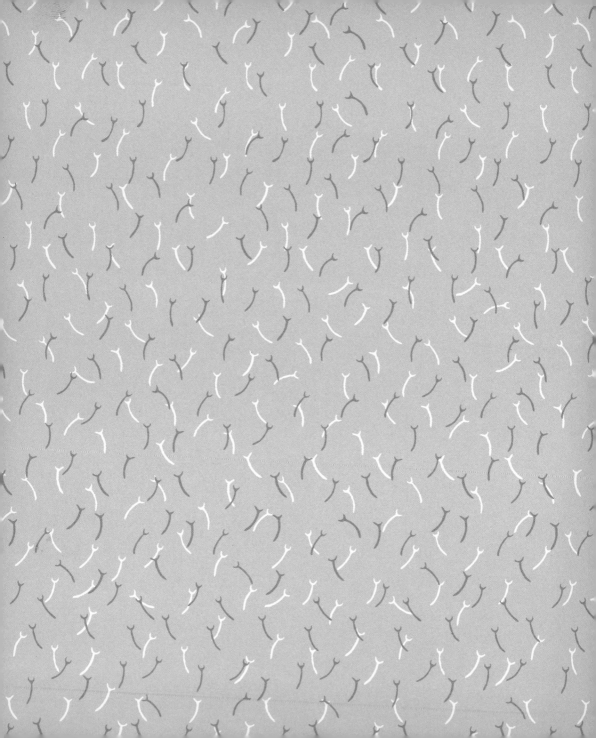

ONCE UPON A TIMELESS TALE

The Princess and the Pea

STORY BY **HANS CHRISTIAN ANDERSEN**
RETOLD BY **MARGRETE LAMOND**

PICTURES BY
MITCH VANE

LITTLE HARE
www.littleharebooks.com

Once, in a land far away—though not so far away as all that—there lived a handsome prince who would one day be king, but who had a problem: he had never found himself a wife.

'When you are king,' the queen reminded him, 'you will need your own queen to share the throne with you.'

'I know,' said the prince. 'But who should she be?'

'She must be a wise person,' said the old queen.

'And sensible,' said the king.

'And particular,' said the queen.

'And delicate,' said the king.

'She must be a real true princess,' said the queen. 'So you can't marry just anyone.'

'But there is no one like that in this kingdom,' said the prince.

'Then you will have to find her somewhere else,' said the queen.

'But how will I know,' said the prince, 'if a princess is real and true?'

'You will know when you know,' said the queen.

So the prince headed off to find a real true princess.

He travelled through many lands, and across many seas, and for many months. On his travels, he met many women.

Some were young and some were old; some were wise, but most were plain sly. Some were tall and some were short; some were sensible, but most were simply dull. Some were lovely and some were not; some were delicate, but most were plain sickly. One or two even seemed to be quite particular, but it turned out they were just downright fussy.

None of the women was all the things she needed to be.

BLAH BLAH BLAH BLAH

The prince knew what he knew and went home without a real true princess.

Some weeks after his return, there was a storm. It raged all through the day and into the evening, and then it raged on into the night.

There was thunder and lightning and wind and hail, and the windows of the palace rattled and the walls shook.

Around midnight someone knocked at the palace door.

'Who might that be?' said the queen.

'It must be brigands,' said the king.

'Or beggars,' said the prince.

'Will you let me in?' cried a voice. 'Hello? Help!'

'It's a girl!' said the king.

The king and the queen and the prince ran at once to open the door.

Outside was a young woman, drenched to the bone.

Her clothes had once been delicate and magnificent, but now they streamed with water, and she stood in a puddle nearly up to her knees.

'Come in,' said the king. 'What were you *thinking*, going out on a night like this?'

'I was thinking this and that,' said the girl, as sweet as could be, 'but I keep my thoughts to myself.'

'That's very wise,' said the queen. 'But what were you *doing*, going out on a night like this?'

'I was going about my business,' said the girl, as polite as could be, 'but my business is my own.'

'That's very sensible,' said the prince, as he led her to the fire. 'But who *are* you?'

'I am who I am,' said the girl, as modest as could be.

She would tell them no more.

'Well,' whispered the queen to the king, 'her clothes and her manners are fine, but she is drenched to the bone and not even shivering.'

'She must be a peasant,' the king whispered back. 'For a moment I thought she might be a real true princess, but now I'm not so sure.'

'We shall have to see what we see,' said the queen.

The prince, however, didn't care if the girl was princess or peasant. He had fallen in love with her.

'You must stay here tonight,' he told her.

The queen didn't want the prince to fall in love with a girl who wasn't a real true princess, so she decided to set a test. She went to the guest chamber to prepare a bed. First she placed a dried pea on the bare bed-boards, and then she piled twenty straw mattresses on top. On top of the straw mattresses, she piled twenty mattresses filled with feathers.

'We'll find out if she's a real true princess,' the queen said to the king.

When it was time to sleep, the girl was not the least dismayed to see such a high bed with so many mattresses.

She climbed the ladder and snuggled under the eiderdown.

Meanwhile, the storm raged on. It was so wild that the king didn't sleep, but tossed and turned all night. The queen didn't sleep either. She was so busy wondering about the pea that she, too, tossed and turned. It was the same for the prince—he was so in love with the girl that he couldn't even close his eyes.

As for the girl, she tossed and turned and twisted and squirmed on top of her forty mattresses, all the long night through.

She never slept a wink.

'How did you sleep?' the queen asked her in the morning.

'I confess I didn't sleep at all,' said the girl, as tired as could be.

'Was it the storm?' asked the king.

'Was it your thoughts?' asked the prince.

'I hope it wasn't the bed,' said the queen.

'I confess it might have been the bed,' said the girl, as truthful as could be. 'There was something hard under the mattress, and I am bruised all over.'

The queen winked at the king, and the king winked back.

They knew what they knew: that only a real true princess could be as particular as to feel a pea buried under forty mattresses.

The prince knew what he knew, too, and he and the girl were married—if not the very next day, then probably the very day after.

As for the pea, it was put on display so everybody could see it for themselves. It is still there—if no one has stolen it—because believe it or not, this is a true story.

Little Hare Books
an imprint of
Hardie Grant Egmont
Ground Floor, Building 1, 658 Church Street
Richmond, Victoria 3121, Australia

www.littleharebooks.com

Text copyright © Little Hare Books 2014
Text by Margrete Lamond
Illustrations copyright © Mitch Vane 2014

First published 2014

Cataloguing-in-Publication details are available from the
National Library of Australia

978 1 921894 93 0 (hbk.)

Designed by Vida & Luke Kelly
Produced by Pica Digital, Singapore
Printed in China by Wai Man Book Binding Ltd.

5 4 3 2 1

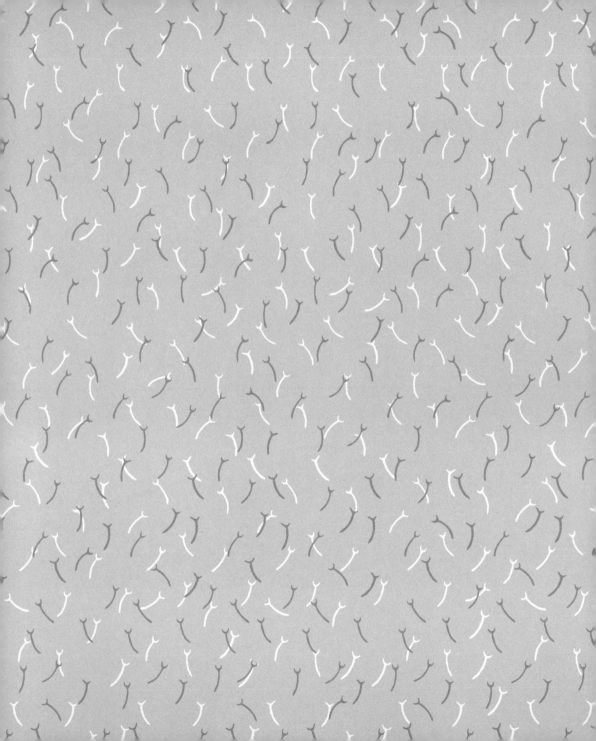

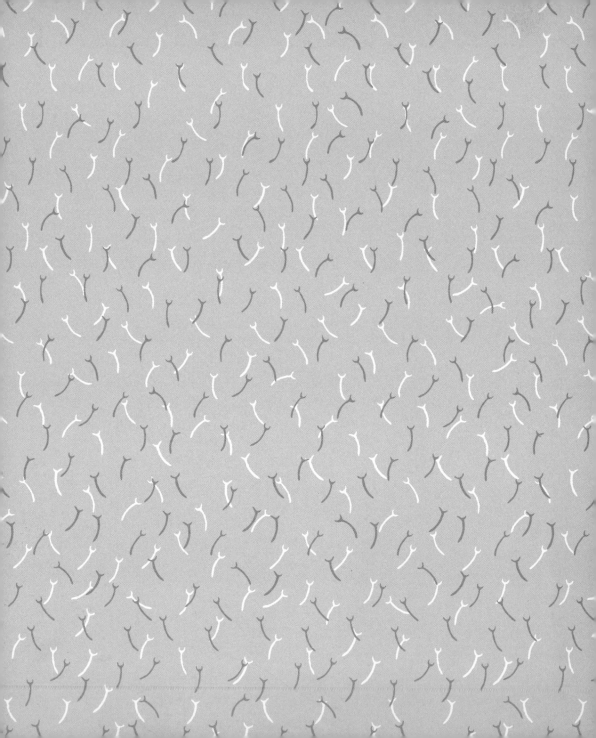